HENRY

JAMES

PERCY

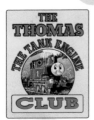
First published in Great Britain 1993 by Buzz Books,
an imprint of Reed International Books Ltd
Michelin House, 81 Fulham Road, London SW3 6RB
and Auckland, Melbourne, Singapore and Toronto

ISBN 1 85591 291 0

Printed in Italy by Olivotto

TIME FOR TROUBLE

buzz books

The Island of Sodor had many visitors and the Fat Controller had scheduled more trains. Gordon, the big engine, had to work harder than ever before.

"Come on," he called to the coaches. "Come on, come on, come on. The passengers rely on me to be on time."

Whenever Gordon finished one journey, it was time for another to begin.

"Never mind," he puffed. "I like a good long run to stretch my wheels."

Even so, the Fat Controller decided that Gordon needed a rest.

"James shall do your work."

James was delighted. He liked to show off his smart red paint, and he was determined to be as fast as Gordon.

"You know, little Toby," he boasted. "I'm an important engine. Everyone knows it. I'm as regular as clockwork. Never late, always on time."

"Says you," replied Toby.

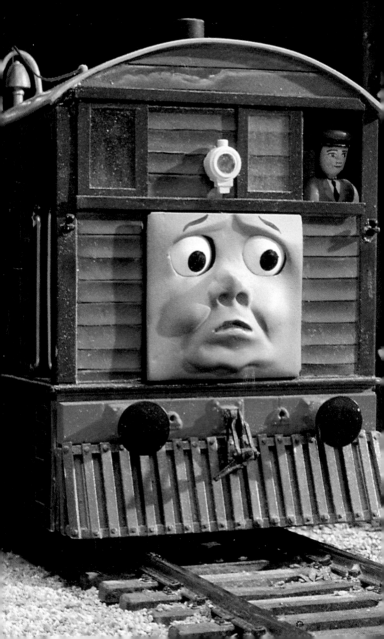

Just then the Fat Controller arrived.

"Your parts are worn, Toby, so you must go to the works to be mended."

"Can I take Henrietta, Sir?"

"No, what would the passengers do without her?"

Toby saw Percy by the water tower.
"Don't worry, Toby,." said Percy. "I'll take care of Henrietta until you get back."

Soon Toby was out on the main line.
He clanked as he trundled along.

He's a little engine with small wheels.
His tanks don't hold much water. He had
come a long way and began to feel thirsty.

In the distance was a signal.

"Good," he thought, "there's a station ahead. I can have a nice drink and a rest until James has passed."

Toby's driver thought so, too.

Toby was enjoying his drink when the
signalman came up. He had never seen
Toby before. Toby's driver tried to explain,
but the new signalman wouldn't listen.

"We must clear the line for James with
the express. You'll have to get more water
at the next station."

Toby clanked sadly away.

Hurrying used a lot of water and his tanks were soon empty.

Poor Toby was out of steam and stranded on the main line!

"We must warn James," said the fireman.

Then he saw Percy and Henrietta.

"Please take me back to the station. It's an emergency."

Henrietta hated leaving Toby.

"Never mind," said Percy. "You're taking the fireman to warn James. That's a big help."

Henrietta felt much better.

James was fuming when he heard the news. "I'm going to be late."

"My fault," said the signalman. "I didn't understand about Toby."

"Now James," said his driver, "you'll have to push Toby."

"What, me? Me, push Toby and pull my train, too!"

Grumbling dreadfully, James set off to find Toby.

He came up behind Toby and gave him a bump. "Get on, you."

James had to work very hard. When he reached the works station, he felt exhausted.

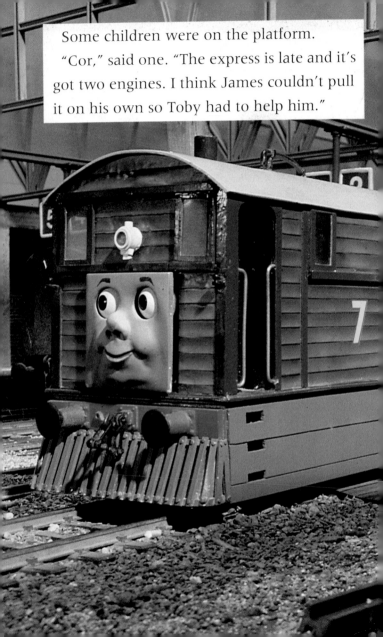

Some children were on the platform.

"Cor," said one. "The express is late and it's got two engines. I think James couldn't pull it on his own so Toby had to help him."

"Never mind, James," whispered Toby. "They're only joking."

"Hah-hah," said James.

THOMAS

EDWARD

GORDON